This book belongs to:

....

....

....

Retold by Gaby Goldsack
Illustrated by Emma Lake
Designed by Jester Designs

Language consultant: Betty Root

ISBN 978-1-4075-0356-1

This edition published by Parragon in 2007

Parragon Publishing
Queen Street House
4 Queen Street
Bath BA1 1HE, UK

Printed in Indonesia

p

The Three Little Pigs

Helping Your Child Read

Learning to read is an exciting challenge for most children. From a very early age, sharing story books with children, talking about the pictures and guessing what might happen next are all very important parts of the reading experience.

Sharing reading

Set aside a regular quiet time to share reading with younger children, or to be on hand to encourage older children as they develop into independent readers.

First Readers are intended to encourage and support the early stages of learning to read. They present well-loved tales that children will enjoy hearing again and again. Familiarity helps children to identify some of the words and phrases.

When you feel your child is ready to move ahead, encourage him or her to join in so that you read the story aloud together. Always pause to talk about the pictures. The easy-to-read speech bubbles in **First Readers** provide an excellent 'joining-in' activity. The bright, clear illustrations and matching text will help children to understand the story.

Building confidence

In time, children will want to read *to* you. When this happens, be patient and give continual praise. They may not read all the words correctly, but children's substitutions are often very good guesses.

The repetition in each book is particularly helpful for building confidence. If your child cannot read a particular word, go back to the beginning of the sentence and read it together so the meaning is not lost. Most important, do not continue if your child is tired or just needs a break.

Reading alone

The next step is to ask your child to read alone. Try to be on hand to give help and support. Remember to give lots of encouragement and praise.

Along with other simple stories, **First Readers** will ensure that children will find reading an enjoyable and rewarding experience.

Off we go!

Once upon a time there were three little pigs who lived in the woods. There were two brothers and a sister.

A big bad wolf lived in the woods too. So one day the three little pigs set off to find new homes.

Soon the three little pigs saw a pile of straw.

"I'll build my house with straw," said the first little pig.

The two little pigs walked on. They saw a pile of sticks.

"I'll build my house with sticks," said the second little pig.

The third little pig walked on.
She saw a pile of bricks.
"I'll build a strong house with bricks," said the third little pig.

It took her a very long time. Her brothers laughed at her for working so hard. But her house of bricks was very strong.

The very next day, the big bad wolf came to the house of straw. He was dressed as an old woman.

"Little pig, little pig, let me in," said the wolf.

But the first little pig saw that it was the wolf.

He said, "Not by the hair of my chinny chin chin."

So the wolf huffed, and he puffed, and he blew the house down.

The little pig ran away. He hid with his brother in the house of sticks.

The next day, the big bad wolf came to the house of sticks. He was dressed as a sheep. "Little pig, little pig, let me in," said the wolf.

But the second little pig saw that it was the wolf. He said, "Not by the hair of my chinny chin chin."

So the wolf huffed, and he puffed, and he blew the house down.

So the two little pigs ran away. They hid with their sister in her house of bricks.

But the next day the big bad wolf came to the house of bricks.
"Little pig, little pig, let me in," said the wolf.

And the third little pig said, "Not by the hair of my chinny chin chin."

So the wolf huffed, and he puffed, and he puffed, and he huffed. But he could not blow the house down.

"Let me in!" cried the wolf.

But the third little pig still would not let him in.

The big bad wolf was very angry. "I'm coming down the chimney to eat you up," he cried.

The first two little pigs were very scared. But the third little pig made a big fire under the chimney. Then she put a big pot of water on the fire.

The big bad wolf climbed into the chimney. The first two little pigs hid under the table.

The big bad wolf slid down the chimney. The first two little pigs shut their eyes.

Then, splash! The big bad wolf fell into the pot of hot water.

"Help! Help!" cried the wolf.
He jumped out of the pot and
ran out of the house.

The three little pigs jumped for joy. And they never saw that big bad wolf again.

Read and Say

How many of these words can you say? The pictures will help you. Look back in your book and see if you can find the words in the story.

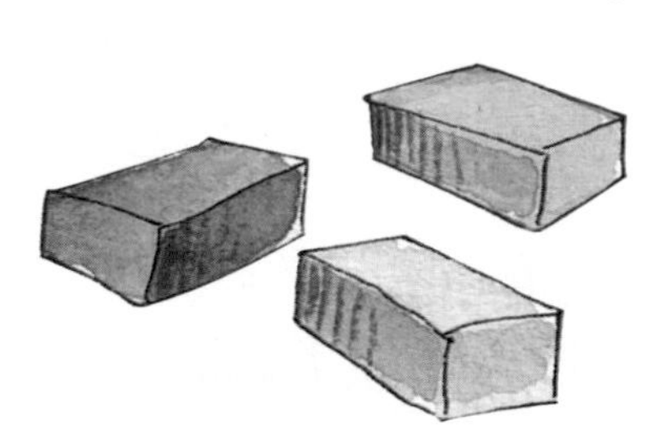

bricks

chimney

fire

house

pigs

pot

sticks

straw

table

wolf